The Awakening

The Way to Freedom

Book 3

H.M. Clarke

Also by H.M.Clarke

The Way to Freedom Series
1: The Kalarthri
1.1: The Cavern of Sethi
2: The Dream Thief
3. The Awakening
4. The Enemy Within
5. The Unknown Queen
6. The Searchers
7. The Whisperer
8. The Deceiver
9. The Great Game
10. The Gathering
The Complete Season One – Books 1-5

Coming soon
The Complete Season Two – Books 6-10

John McCall Mysteries
1: Howling Vengeance

The Verge
1: The Enclave

Coming Soon
2: Citizen Erased

The Order
1: Winter's Magic
Marion: An 'Order' Short Story

The Awakening

The Way to Freedom

Book 3

H.M. Clarke

Sentinel Publishing

First published in The United States of America in 2014
Second edition published in The United States of America in 2019

Sentinel Publishing LLC, Dayton, Ohio

Cover design by DerrangedDoctorDesign

DEDICATION

As always, this book is dedicated to my two beautiful children, Keith and Ariadne.

CONTENTS

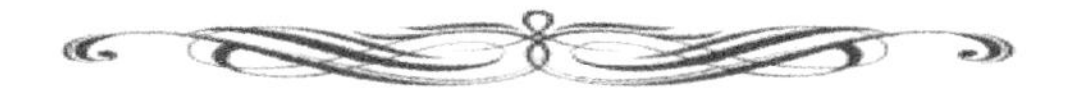

Trust.

Hard to win,

Easy to lose,

And never to be taken lightly.

-Suenese Proverb

CHAPTER ONE

THE MISSING

Vosloo was furious.

The anger he felt this morning was nothing compared to what he felt now. The Captain slammed his fist into the earth and watched as the footprint he was examining disappeared into a fine spray of dust.

Sitting back on his haunches, Vosloo again studied the grasslands about him. The long grass bobbed peacefully in the breeze and to the northwest, he could see the dark smudge of green where the forest started to tumble from the foothills of the ranges.

A small distance away from him was the hunched form of Adhamh who had woken from unconsciousness not long after he did. The Hatar's usually glossy feathers now looked dull and lifeless, as if all the vigor and substance had been drained from them. The creature's head also swung back and forth as if trapped in a trance. Vosloo knew that Adhamh was trying to sense where Kalena was located.

The Wing Commander was missing when

Vosloo awoke with a blinding headache and the smell of his own blood flooding his nostrils. The sight of the neatly cut leg straps told him that Kalena had been taken. From the blood that was smeared across the saddle and Adhamh's neck feathers, she would have been injured and most probably unconscious.

The Captain groaned as he looked up into the sky. The position of the sun showed that they had been out for a good part of the day.

The Captain then unbuckled his own leg straps and slipped down from Adhamh's back to the earth below. He kept a good grip on the Hatar's feathers as a dizzy spell quickly came over him. Vosloo touched a hand to his face and it came back covered in blood.

Now that he was thinking of it, Vosloo could feel the throbbing of the cut on his forehead. He then vaguely remembered his head hitting the back of Kalena's helmet when he was thrown forward. He remembered nothing after that. Vosloo unbuckled his helmet and dropped it unnoticed to the ground.

Once he was sure the dizziness had gone, Vosloo started to work carefully around the unconscious Hatar. Vosloo could see that Adhamh still drew breath but did not want to try and wake him until he found out more about what happened. Not that the Hatar could converse with him, but he could definitely listen.

They had crashed into the grasslands, leaving a large furrow in their wake. Amazingly

Adhamh showed no signs of physical injury from the crash that Vosloo could see. The furrow itself did not look natural, it was crisply cut and symmetrical as if someone had pressed a large cylinder into soft sand. But the Captain put it from his mind as he saw what was in the dirt that was kicked up from their impact.

Around Adhamh's body was a myriad of tracks and on closer inspection, Vosloo determined that they were those of Icetigers. There could be no mistake with pads larger than a human fist and claws big enough to gut a man. And there were enough tracks to tell Vosloo that there had been at least four of the creatures crawling around them as they slept.

"Blast everything to Bellus and back," he

shouted in frustration. Cursing, even more, Vosloo got to his feet and marched over to Adhamh. The Hatar swung his head down to look the Captain in the face with one cat slit eye. Even Vosloo's fury could not stop him from shuddering slightly when the Hatar's three eyelids blinked quickly in succession as it gazed at him.

"She's gone. Taken by those cursed Icetigers. Their tracks disappear into the grasslands towards the foothills. I can't track them." Vosloo went to push his fingers through his hair but remembered his cut forehead as the tips of his fingers touched the scab. His fingers came away covered in dried blood flakes.

"Can you hear her?" Vosloo asked as he began to scrub at the dried blood on his cheeks.

The Hatar stilled for a moment but shook his head.

"No, of course not. If you could you'd be after her already."

Adhamh nodded agreement and then swung his head around and looked to the West.

"Why didn't they just kill us. Why did they just take her? Unless they know." Vosloo knew as he spoke that it was impossible for them to know. Only a hand full of people knew Kalena's secret.

Adhamh's head swung quickly around to look at the Captain and Vosloo nearly took a step backward at the menace he felt coming from the Hatar. His frustration was getting the better of him and he had let his mouth wander. Then to the west, Vosloo saw a glint in the sky.

"What is that?" Vosloo quickly pointed and Adhamh turned his attention to the west. The glint grew stronger and was quickly joined by others.

Then Adhamh suddenly rose to his haunches and bellowed.

The sound deafened Vosloo and he could feel the noise vibrate through the earth. Then faintly, he heard an answering bellow coming from the west. The rest of the Wing had found them, now there might be a chance of getting Kalena back. If they do not then their plans for the last eighteen years would be lost with no hope of completion. Prince Garrick will need to be told.

Vosloo watched the Hatar who was still sitting back on his haunches and gave a small prayer of thanks to the One for his luck. Hopefully,

Adhamh will not remember his little slip of the tongue.

At least this incident should keep the Justicars off his back. *'Inman the little turd thinks he can either control me or condemn me,'* Vosloo thought. The meeting he had with the blonde Justicar that morning told him as much. *'The little bastard thought he could blackmail me with innuendo and rumor. Well, he had another thing coming!'*

Vosloo sat himself down on the grass. It would be some time before the Wing arrives, and it looked to Vosloo as if Adhamh was already filling the approaching Hatar in on what had happened.

He could wait. Vosloo was an expert at waiting.

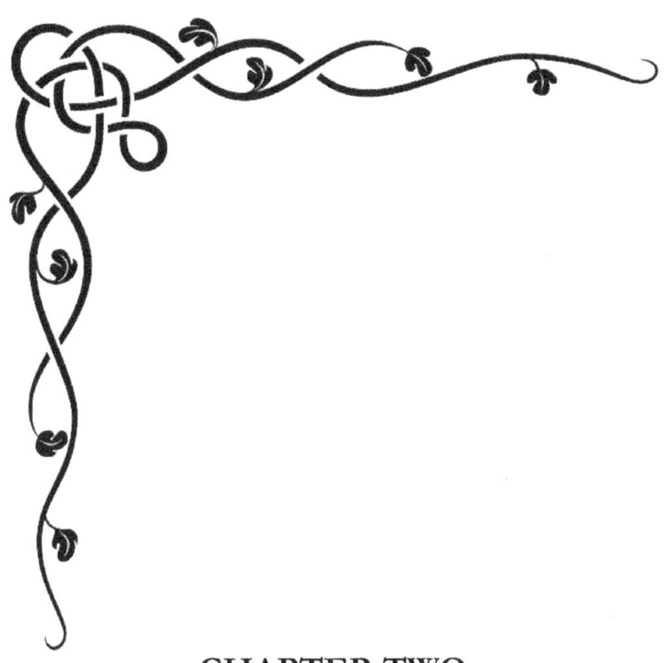

CHAPTER TWO

NEWS

'Wing Commander Adhamh is just ahead of us on the plains,' Trar relayed to Tayme. *'Adhamh also says that they have lost Wing Commander Kalena.'*

'Lost. What does he mean by lost?' Tayme tried not to let the desperation he felt show in his

mind voice. The Wing had lost contact with Wing Commanders' Adhamh and Kalena for most of the day. When they were not at the rendezvous point, Tayme and Lunman organized the Wing into search parties to look for them.

They had been searching for several hours when the Hatar heard Adhamh's mental call. Then Trar, as the senior Hatar became the main relay between Adhamh and the Wing.

'That's all the Wing Commander told me Tayme. You might have to get your answers from Captain Vosloo, though ...' Trar stopped speaking as if trying to order her thoughts. *'The Wing Commander warned us to be careful around the Captain. Adhamh does not trust him.'*

'If he's talking then she's-'

'Not dead,' Trar interrupted *'If she was deceased then the Wing Commander would have said so. She is 'just lost.'*

'Did Adhamh tell you anything about what happened?' Tayme could now see the small black figure of the Wing Commander against the rippling green of the grasslands. Behind him was a deep red scar, as if a giant plough had tried to make a furrow in the turf.

The Hatar had crashed landed but why?

'They were hit by a Mind Bolt from the ground. They were chased from the mountains by it.'

'Mind Bolts?' Tayme felt a shiver go down his spine. He had seen Hatar hunting birds with Mind Bolts; it was not a pretty sight. Tayme

quickly glanced around him at the Hatar flying in tight formation.

'Trar, command the wing to fan out. We do not want to present a bunched target in case the bastards are still waiting below us.'

Trar relayed the order and slowly the Wing began to drift apart into a staggered line too wide for any Mind Bolt to hit. When the Wing was settled into its new formation, Tayme bent his mind back to information gathering.

'Trar, what is this about not trusting the Captain?'

The Hatar gave Tayme a mental shrug. *'I do not know. Adhamh just said that he did not trust the man and that we should not trust everything he says.'*

Tayme's mind reeled at this revelation. Why would Adhamh not trust a man that spoke of rebellion? The Captain is also a man that Harada trusted. What happened to make Adhamh lose his trust in him?

'Speak to the Captain first when we get there. I am sure that Adhamh will speak to us privately when he is able.'

'Can Adhamh even talk to Kalena?'

'He has not told me. We will find out when we get there.'

Tayme clamped down on his frustration. It would be no use ranting against Trar; he would just have to wait.

Tayme knew he was not good at waiting.

CHAPTER THREE

IN THE GRASSLANDS

Tayme just did not believe it.

"Are you telling me that Wing Commander Kalena was taken by the Icetigers from the saddle in front of you without killing both yourself and Adhamh?"

Even when he said it himself it still could

not be believed.

Captain Vosloo jerked his head in agreement but Tayme noticed that his hands were bunched into fists at his sides as if he was trying to keep his temper in check.

Before landing the Wing, Tayme had sent four Flyers to search the North-Eastern grasslands and foothills on the information that Adhamh had passed to Trar. But the story he had just heard from the Captain sounded unbelievable. Why were they left alive? Why was only the Wing Commander taken? If it were to have an officer as a hostage, surely Captain Fraser Vosloo would have been a better option.

But there was no mistaking the very real evidence of Tiger tracks in the ploughed up earth and the missing Wing Commander.

Since landing Second Lieutenant Holm Lunman had not said a word. He just stood one step away from Tayme looking carefully at the site where Adhamh had crashed landed.

"How would they know who they were as Adhamh is not the only black Hatar in the Wings. And if they were after Kalena, how would they know that she would be here at this exact moment?" Lunman slowly said as his gaze was drawn again to the foothills. "Maybe it wasn't the Wing Commander they were after. Maybe they just wanted a Flyer."

"What do you mean?" Tayme looked in the same direction as Lunman to see if he could gain a clue to the man's thinking.

"Perhaps they just wanted to get their hands on a Flyer to see how we 'work' and the Tigers took the Wing Commander because she is easier to carry than Adhamh."

"You think that they want to experiment on the Wing Commander?" Tayme said in disbelief.

"It was just a possibility." Lunman turned to look Tayme in the face. "It is better than thinking her dead already."

"Perhaps they think she can report on the Wings movements. Perhaps the Tigers think that we can all hear each other?"

"A message needs to be sent to Prince Garrick at Darkon immediately telling him of these events," Captain Vosloo said hurriedly drawing the eyes of both the Wing Lieutenants. From his face and the sudden set of his posture, Tayme knew the Captain had quickly made some kind of decision.

"Wing Lieutenant Tayme, as you are the senior Lieutenant, I am promoting you to Acting Wing Commander until Kalena is found."

"Yes, Sir." Tayme snapped to attention straight away.

"Pick your fastest pair and have them come and see me. I will give them a verbal message that needs to be delivered to Prince Garrick at all costs."

"Yes, sir."

'Trar, tell Bayla to get Tom and report to the Captain-'

'I have already talked to Bayla. They flew out on the search for Kalena but they are on their way back now.'

'Thanks Trar.'

"Our fastest Flyer is on her way and Tom is a man who can be trusted to get the message through."

"Good. Once they are on their way we will head back to the column and report what has happened to the Black Robes-"

"What about the Wing Commander?" Tayme asked through gritted teeth. He could not believe that the Captain would just leave Kalena to her fate. Tayme could not allow that to happen. He had heard the tales that swept Darkon before they came north about how Icetiger treat their hostages and prisoners. Victims were mangled and disemboweled and then left to freeze solid in the harsh snows of winter while their last breath was escaping their lungs. Many people had been found like this. Tayme had even heard that Vosloo himself had led a rescue squad out of Fort Foxtern after a group of Tigers took one of his soldiers.

Once Tom and Bayla are on their way to Darkon with their message, Tayme and three other riders were going to go after Kalena. Lunman can escort the Captain back and let him explain to Harada what had happened.

"As soon as our reports are made and we provision those selected from the Wing to go then we will come back and begin our search-"

"The trail will be cold by then Captain," Tayme quickly replied. Beside him, Lunman moved uneasily on his feet.

"Everything about the IceTigers is cold

Tayme," the Captain said, a small smile playing about his lips. "If the Hatar are as good at scouting as Kalena has told me, then we should be able to find her. And we *do* need to find her."

The last statement caught Tayme's attention and he cast a questioning gaze at the Captain as thoughts came unbidden to his mind. What stake does the Captain have in Kalena? A twinge of jealously rippled through Tayme's body and he did with it as he had always in the past. He buried it deep inside his mind and told himself not to be a fool. The man had only known Kalena for a week.

Tayme rubbed a hand through his hair and grimaced at the feel of the sweat and dirt that was caked in it. He could live with it for a few more days or however long it would take to find her.

"It might be too late for her by then Captain."

Captain Vosloo turned to stare at him, his face and eyes were now unreadable. Tayme stared back at him. The large purple birthmark that covered half of his face would usually make people turn their eyes away from his, as if afraid that the mark could travel across his gaze and set up residence on their own body. The only person who had never ever turned from his gaze was Kalena. As a child, she had always accepted him and never shunned him as the other new Flyers had.

Fraser Vosloo did not disappoint him. The Captain held his gaze longer than most but his eyes still slid away from Tayme's face to stare at a point just behind him. Tayme tried not to smile. He felt as if he had won a small victory and it sated his small jealous monster for the moment.

"Very well. Organize a small party to join those who are already searching." The Captain paused and a small smile began to play at his lips again. "You will be leaving Lieutenant Lunman in charge while you are away?"

Tayme nodded.

"Send word back as soon as you find her. And I think you should take Adhamh with you, he's the best thing we have to locate her."

"I was planning to Captain. It would be the worst thing we can do to not to involve him"

And Tayme wanted to be able to talk in private with the Hatar. There was something strange happening here that he could not quite put his finger on and Tayme wanted to get to the bottom

of it.

CHAPTER FOUR

WILLARD MALCHANCE

Prince Garrick Thurad had just finished his breakfast when he heard the timid knock at the door to his suite. He wiped away the breakfast crumbs from his mouth with his napkin as a servant moved to open the door.

At least now he did not have to worry about

Felian pestering and whining to him about what she thinks he should and should not do. Garrick's last straw regarding Felian was broken when, on the night of the war meeting, his father's mistress tried to turn her seductions onto him. Felian is a beautiful woman to look at but Garrick knew that her soul is black and dead of joy and was repulsed by her.

She had crawled uninvited into his bed while he slept and – Garrick could not even think of what she tried to do and he shivered in remembered revulsion. He had thrown her out of his bed and yelled at her to leave his rooms immediately. The woman had quickly picked up the flimsy robe she had worn and scuttled as quickly as she could through his outer rooms and vanished naked into the hallway. By the One's sake, she was supposed to be carrying his father's child (though Garrick did not believe one word of that). The next morning she had left Darkon to go back to Hered where even now she would be whispering lies into his father's ear. But he should not be thinking of her – at least not today.

Murmuring at the door resolved itself into the large form of Garrick's Chief Advisor, Lord Willard Malchance, Duke of Morcar. He had arrived from the Capital a day after his father's mistress left for it. The news he had bought with him was not good. Garrick's father had collapsed again into another illness. This time the court Physicians did not think he would recover.

Malchance had made sure that there were Physicians in Garrick's pay attending him. Both had worried that lately, the Emperor had fallen ill to many times to be judged 'natural'.

Garrick rose from the table to greet his friend with a warm smile. "Good Morning Malchance, if you were a little earlier we could have broken our fast together."

"Thank you for the offer Your Grace but you know that I do not eat on a sleepy stomach."

Garrick laughed and clapped a hand on the Duke's shoulder. Garrick had never known Malchance to eat anything before noon. The man had always said that to eat early was to slow a man down. The Duke of Morcar is a tall, well built man in his late thirties with thick dark hair and neatly clipped black beard. Today, as always, he was dressed in the finest materials that had been tailored into a simple court style.

Garrick gestured for the Duke to take a seat opposite at his breakfast table and both men then sat down in the comfortable padded chairs. After a moment Garrick waved to his servants to clear away his breakfast dishes.

Once this was done he issued an order to be left alone. Once the last man had gone Garrick's stiff frame slumped into his chair and the forced cheerfulness he had been exhibiting all morning fell away.

"What brings you here so early, Wil?" Garrick asked as he refilled his goblet with mulled wine and then offered some to Malchance.

The Duke shook his head slightly at the offer. "I thought you could do with the company this morning considering what day this is."

Garrick's mouth set in a tight line as the image of pale flesh covered in a tangle of long, dark hair flashed before his eyes. He drained the contents of his goblet and briefly considered refilling it before placing it back empty on the table.

"Caitlin was too young to die," Garrick murmured.

"Of course she was and we all know who orchestrated it don't we," Malchance leaned forward in his chair, the fury clearly seen blazing in his eyes.

"Please. Not today. Do not mention that woman's name aloud today." Garrick was already ashamed of his earlier thoughts on that woman.

Malchance settled back in his chair as

Garrick raised a finger in warning.

"Very well, I won't. But it galls me that she still walks this earth while my sister Caitlin lies beneath it."

Garrick's anger at Malchance suddenly evaporated. It was very easy to forget that others, as well as himself, loved Caitlin.

"Stay with me today Wil so we can talk about old times. I think both of us do not wish to be left alone on the Anniversary of Caitin's death."

Garrick poured himself another goblet of wine and sat back in his chair. He held the cup close to his chest where the warmth of the wine penetrated the gloom that had descended around them.

Both men sat in silence with their thoughts.

Garrick and Caitlin were both very young when they married. They had only just turned fifteen. The ink had not quite dried on the marriage contracts when Caitlin fell pregnant on their wedding night. The next nine months were the happiest in his life, and then Caitlin died in childbirth. He was grief-stricken at the news but was filled with hope when the midwife told him that his daughter still lived.

Malchance who was with him while he waited suddenly stormed into the birth chamber and lifted the swaddled baby from the arms of the Emperor's new mistress – Felian. He then carried her out to meet her father. Glancing briefly at his daughter to reassure himself that she lived, Garrick then entered the chamber with the midwife protesting and imploring him to wait until the Princess Caitlin had been made presentable.

Garrick ignored her and burst into the room to see Caitlin's pale flesh smeared with blood and her long black hair was tangled in sweat and tears.

Garrick dragged his thoughts away from that single moment. It was at that moment that he knew his wife had not died a natural death. His brother-in-law had never liked his father's mistress and already thought she was involved with the death of Garrick's mother only a few months before. It was that night that both Garrick and Malchance began to formulate the plan for the hiding of this delicate, beautiful, perfect little baby, (Garrick could not help but smile at the thought of his daughter), from the machinations of Felian.

The problem was that it had never seemed safe to bring her back to her true family until it was too late to do anything without showing their hand to their enemies.

"How is Kalena?" Malchance knew what was on his mind.

"She has grown to be the spitting image of her mother Wil. Did you know that she is a Wing Commander now?" Garrick could not help the pride in his voice. Both his brother and his daughter are Wing Commanders. "Provost Marshall Brock has sent her Wing North with that of Harada's."

"Was letting her go really a good idea?" The concern Malchance felt for a niece he had not seen in eighteen years was clear in the man's voice.

“Harada is with her. He’ll make sure that nothing happens to her. Also, Fraser Vosloo is flying with her as added protection. I have placed Fraser in direct command of the two Wings to ensure that they are protected.”

“I had heard last night that you had pissed off the two Justicars that are with the freemen army by making Vosloo and the Wings independent from their control.” A sly grin showed through Malchance’s black beard.

“Yes. Inman was not happy about it. But I am worried about the second Justicar.” Garrick took a sip from his goblet and grimaced. The mulled wine had gone cold.

“Why? From what I understand he is only Inman’s new lackey.” Malchance must have noticed Garrick's grimace as he reached across and took the nearly empty wine pitcher as he spoke. He then got up and went to the fire to refill the pitcher from the wine pot that was warming on the hearth.

"Inman's new 'lackey' just happens to be Videan Tsarland, Kalena's foster brother," Garrick said as he placed his goblet on the table and slouched further into his chair.

"Does he know anything?" The Duke placed the wine ladle back into the pot and carried the newly filled pitcher back to the table.

"If he does he has given no indication of it." Malchance seated himself at the table and poured himself a cup of the mulled wine. "If Inman hasn't shown any knowledge of who Kalena really is then maybe this Videan doesn't know anything." The

Duke took a quick swig of his drink. "As far as anyone is concerned, the official version is that Kalena Thurad, your Royal daughter, has been fostered to live with my uncle in Istay to learn the countries language and customs."

"That fabrication cannot last forever. She is now eighteen years old and should by rights be on her way back to Suene to take her rightful place as my heir. But that cannot happen, not until I have neutralized Felian and all her cur supporters."

"You have asked Vosloo to keep an eye on Videan then?" Malchance shifted in his chair. Malchance had never really got on well with Fraser Vosloo, especially after the Captain's sister died. It wasn't anything personal; it was just that the Duke did not like the man.

"Yes, I have."

"Is that wise considering Inman-"

"Leave it be Wil. Fraser has promised me that Inman will not cloud his reasoning."

Malchance quickly closed his mouth on what he was about to say and sat staring across the table at Garrick. Garrick ignored his friend's scrutiny and quickly tossed back the rest of his cold wine and rose from the table to perch on the window ledge to look down onto the manicured lawns three storey's below.

"Garrick, will you stick with the plans we started eighteen years ago today?"

Malchance's voice was so quiet that Garrick barely heard it. What they had begun to plan so long ago had now evolved from just trying to protect his young daughter to a family betrayal against his father. A fate that he was forced into by his father's unwillingness to see what was happening around him.

Garrick turned hardened eyes to look at Malchance.

"I have already desecrated the sacred law by allowing my first born child to become a Hatar Kalar Wil. I will not stop now until I am Emperor and Kalena and all her kind is freed."

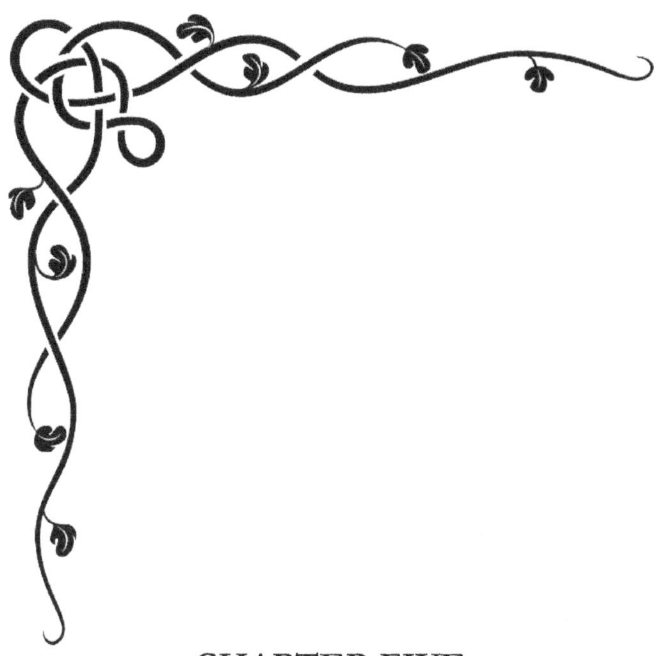

CHAPTER FIVE

THE MESSENGER ARRIVES

Frantic knocking at the door interrupted the two men.

Garrick grimaced in annoyance while Malchance lifted himself from his chair and quickly opened the door to see who would interrupt the two men after Prince Garrick had asked to be left alone.

After a few moments of whispered speech at the door, the Duke of Morcar turned worried eyes towards his Prince.

"You Grace, there is a Hatar Kalar downstairs with a message that he has been instructed only to speak to your ears alone."

"A Hatar Kalar?" Garrick slowly rose from the windowsill. "What Wing are they from?"

Malchance hesitated a moment before replying, unsure of what to say. "He's from Second Wing, Second Flight Your Grace."

"He?" Hopes that it was Kalena downstairs was dashed. Garrick knew his disappointment sounded clear in his voice. He quickly banished his regret. "Wil, have him bought up to see me straight away."

Malchance nodded and turned and murmured again to the man waiting in the corridor. Then he closed the door on the man's retreating footsteps. The worry had not left the Duke's face.

"What else did you hear Wil?"

Malchance stayed standing near the door, his hand resting on the handle. "The man and his beast have flown over sixteen hours non-stop to get here. The Hatar collapsed exhausted on the landing field and apparently the man looks to have been dragged through death and back. He's nearly killed himself bringing you whatever it is he's carrying."

At the Duke's words, Garrick felt a warning premonition run through his body. His eyes glazed over and he saw again the flash of pale flesh and tangled black hair. But this time he knew it was not

Caitin. Garrick blinked and the vision disappeared and he turned distraught eyes to Malchance.

"Something has happened to Kalena."

As Garrick spoke there was a single rap at the door and Malchance immediately opened the door to admit the waiting Hatar Kalar.

The man slowly walked across the threshold and Garrick could see it was only the Kalar's force of will that was keeping the man upright. He was covered from head to feet in fine red dust that had clotted in the moisture about his eyes, nose, and mouth. Exhaustion dripped from his body and Garrick could plainly see the blood caked lacerations inflicted on hands and face.

The Kalar must have hung on for dear life, collecting every grain of dirt and flying insect in the sky as the Hatar flew as fast as it was able to get to Darkon.

Bloodshot eyes looked to Malchance and then, slowly, drifted to Garrick.

"My Prince…" the Kalar's grating voice cracked and failed.

Garrick stepped forward towards the fellow, grabbing his breakfast chair as he passed and carried it quickly over to the Kalar. The man weakly shook his head in protest but the Prince ignored him and, with the help of Malchance, forced the man to sit down.

"Wil, Fetch the man a cup of water."

Malchance crossed to the sideboard and poured a small cup of water from the bronze pitcher before bringing it back. The Duke then helped the man to hold the cup in his injured hands as he sipped carefully at the precious liquid within.

The liquid had loosened his throat because when he next spoke his voice was more solid and deep.

“Thank you.” He said pushing the cup back into Wil’s hands.

“Your Grace, we have come from the North to deliver a message to you from Captain Vosloo. The Captain enforced to me that I only speak to you alone.”

The Kalar’s eyes flicked from the Prince’s face to Malchance and back again. The whites of his eyes stood out against the dark red dust that caked his face and reminded Garrick of a frightened wide-eyed child.

"You can speak freely in front of the Duke of Morcar. What I hear, he hears."

The man glanced one more time at Malchance, his eyes roaming the duke's face as if inwardly debating whether to doggedly stick to his Captain's orders or not. Abruptly, the man gave a great sigh as he shrugged his shoulders before turning back to the Prince to speak his message.

"We have come directly from the Northern Foothills where my Wing Commanders and Captain Vosloo were knocked from the sky by Icetigers."

Garrick felt the blood drain slowly from his face as he heard these words. He felt afraid to hear the rest of this man's message.

"The Captain wants the other Wings of the Hatar Kalar that are in the South to be warned that the Icetigers attacked using a form of Mind Bolt, the Hatar know what that is, and that the movement of any more Wings to the North should be halted until the source of the Mind Bolts has been destroyed."

The messenger paused to catch his breath and then gestured with his injured hands for another sip of water. Garrick watched as water dribbled from the corners of his mouth, leaving white trails through the dust on his face as it trickled down his chin.

The man pushed the cup back into Malchance's hands and breathed a moan of relief as the cold water penetrated the parched tissues of his throat.

"The Captain said to tell you specifically that Wing Commander Kalena Kalar has been captured by the IceTigers after she was bought down. A rescue party has been sent after her."

"She's what!" Garrick fell backward in shock, hitting the floor with a loud thud. He should have felt pain but suddenly, Garrick's body felt numb all over.

Kalena captured? Garrick could not believe it. Would not believe it. Fraser Vosloo would never have allowed it to happen. This must be some kind of sick joke. It must be. But the image he saw had been of pale flesh and tangled black hair. Garrick's premonitions when they came had never been wrong before.

The loud thud of a door closing caught Garrick's attention and he looked up to see Malchance standing quietly by the door. The chair before him was now empty.

"I have let the poor bastard go to his rest. Once he's had a wash and a good sleep and then some food in his gullet, he'll be fine."

Garrick rose unsteadily from the floor and sat in the vacated and now very dusty breakfast chair. The initial shock had receded now and Garrick rubbed his face with both hands to help him concentrate on the here and now.

"How can a fully grown girl be taken right from under his eyes?" Malchance stormed across the room and then began to pace back and forth across its length, arms crossed behind his back.

Seeing Malchance's anger calmed Garrick. It reminded him of a saying of his father's. Nothing good ever came from choices made in anger.

"How could you entrust her to that man Garrick. You know as well as I do what those mangy curs do to their prisoners."

Garrick remained silent, letting his friend vent his outrage and fear. The Kalar had said that a squad has been sent out after her. If they are quick they could find her before anything happens – they might even be on their way back to the Wing with her now.

The one hope he had was that in his flash of vision, the pale flesh was still living.

CHAPTER SIX

RECRIMINATIONS

Harada stood staring at disbelief at Vosloo.

"Why in the One's name did you do that?" Harada watched as the Captain's silhouette moved a little against the backdrop of the distant fires from the Kalar camp.

"I don't need to explain myself to you,"

Vosloo said, a hard edge to his voice. "Garrick entrusted this to me."

"She's my niece, curse you. By the One, you better explain yourself," Harada hissed furiously. "Again. Why did you send a message directly to my brother?

The Captain had returned to camp long after dusk and after the Wing Physician had cleaned and stitched his wounds, he told Harada the events of the day. Now they stood in the dark scrub surrounding the Hatar camp in an effort to speak privately before they made their report to the Justicars.

Harada could feel Vosloo's heated stare even though he could not see it. The man was angry but more at himself than anyone. After hearing about the attack, the Wing Commander knew he could blame no one but himself. He could have ordered Kalena and her Wing to say safe in Darkon, but Garrick would have none of it. He was proud of Kalena and wanted her to do well up North.

And if things went well, their plans could be put into motion. They had started to prepare the way, but now things had come tumbling down. Harada knew that his questions were not helping, but he had to know why the Captain sent his message.

Vosloo remained silent and for that Harada gave him grudging respect.

"Well. What's done is done." Harada relaxed his stance and broke a twig off of a nearby bush and began to half-heartedly strip the leaves from it.

"Yes. What's done is done." Vosloo turned to look back at the camp.

Harada looked as well. The place was hushed and subdued. It did not have the loud laughter and singing as it had nights previously. The news of the IceTigers use of Mind Bolts had swept through the camp like wildfire and then to hear that one of their own was missing and presumed captured …

Harada tried not to think about it.

"We will not tell them about the message. Hopefully, they do not hear of it." Harada dropped his twig to the ground and rubbed his hands together to get some warmth in them. "We will also not tell them about the Wing Commanders disappearance."

The Captain turned back swiftly to look at Harada. "Why in the One's name not?"

"I do not need to explain my reasoning to you," Harada said with a smile to soften his statement.

"Humph," was all the reply he received.

"We will say that you have sent her and the search party to investigate the source of these Mind Bolts. I really do not want them to know just how important she is to us."

"You mean you don't want word to get back to Felian about how important she is to Garrick."

Harada nodded in the darkness.

"Sending a messenger direct to Prince

Garrick is like waving a big red flag over Kalena's head showing Felian's spies where to look." Vosloo thumped a fist into his thigh in frustration as what he had truly done sank in.

"Very well Harada. I will bow to your judgment as I have always done."

Harada could not tell if the resentment in the Captain's voice was directed at him or the situation. No matter what it was directed at, the Wing Commander ignored it. Vosloo resented the fact that Harada wanted them to approach Inman with this information rather than having the Justicar summoned to the Captain's tent. He wanted Inman to be thrown off guard and having Vosloo come to him rather than the other way around would work to their advantage.

"Well and good then. Let us go and get this over with."

Justicar Banner Inman, a black lounging robe wrapped tightly about his body, sat behind his camp desk. He had not said a word during the Captain's report and now he sat glaring at both Harada and Vosloo.

Harada kept his gaze on the small camp table, a step behind the Captain who as a Freeman had a higher ranking in the eyes of the Justicars. The Wing Commander did not mind. Harada felt uncomfortable enough standing in the middle of the Justicar's command tent without being directly under the ice-cold eyes of Inman. It was the first time he had been here. The taunt black canvas rippled in the night breeze and Harada was conscious of the red dust that they had both tracked over the lush gold carpet.

Vosloo did not appear not to mind, on entering the tent he stamped his boots to shake as much of the dust off as he can. Large black candle stands stood behind the Justicar, their flickering light making Inman's sun bleached blonde hair glow unnaturally again the dark backdrop of the tent.

To Harada, the camp table was the most interesting object in this place. Across the table was strewn numerous papers and scrolls along with a partially unrolled map of the grasslands and the northern foothills. Several small red stones that had been collected from outside were holding down the unrolled section of the map but the harsh red ink from Inman's scratchings did not draw Harada's attention as much as the half opened letter that lay upon it.

The wax seal glinted in the candlelight and Harada could see the impression in it clearly. It was the mark made by his mother's signet ring, a ring now used by his father's whore. Seeing the seal bought unbidden memories to Harada's mind, happy memories of when his mother was young and full of life. This seal was the symbol of the Legal Consort of Suene, but to allow a mistress its use…Harada felt appalled at the thought.

From this angle, Harada could not read the

script but the date was clear. It was written two days ago and to the side of the map was a sheet of Parchment half filled with the Justicar's scrawl. Harada stood staring at the map deep in thought only to be interrupted by the voice of the Justicar.

"What makes you think that I am interested in what happens to those feathered freaks. The Icetigers can kill them all for all I care. The Empire did well enough before we took that Island and we would be much better off if we killed every feathered thing on it."

Inman's voice was soft and lecturing but he meant every single word he said. All Justicars thought that way. They have said the same things about the *Pydarki.* Harada's great great great grandfather had exempted them from the Second

Born Rule in exchange for the secrets of the Krytal.

"You are the Intelligence Officer. Come up with some Intelligence that I can use. It would have been nice to have had some warning of this." The Captain restrained himself from saying any more and Harada was glad of that.

Inman made a show of yawning into his sleeve before moving the papers around on his desk. When he had finished, Felian's letter and his reply were covered.

"As you can see I have no information to give you regarding the Icetigers. But if it makes you feel better, why don't you send out a land search party to find this thing? You would have better luck with that then trusting those feathered lizards."

'Feathered lizards! I'll show him feathered lizards.' Samar's voice blistered into Harada's mind.

'Leave it be Samar. Don't show him anything. Remember he's a Justicar.'

"I just might do that Inman. Thanks for the help." Vosloo said before turning and exiting the tent leaving Harada to beat a hasty retreat after him.

The Wing Commander followed the Captain through the camp until they reached Vosloo's tent. Once inside they both collapsed into camp chairs and laughed to dispel the tension that both men felt. After the laughter had subsided Harada sat forward in his chair, his elbows resting on its rickety arms.

"Inman and Felian have been exchanging correspondence. There was a letter from her on his desk that was not two days old."

Vosloo nodded. "I saw it as well and I was able to read a little of his reply before he covered it. He was reporting to her about our movements and location. I also saw both our names written but I could not read in relation to what."

The chair squeaked as Harada leaned back. "Would he know anything about our plans?"

"Of course he doesn't. Felian just has him watching us because of our relationship to Garrick." Vosloo raised a hand to the bandage around his head.

"Maybe. All the same, I'm going to have Samar keep an eye out tomorrow for the bird that the Justicar is going to send and see if we can intercept it. It would be nice to see exactly what he is telling her."

"Better tell Samar not to eat it." Vosloo laughed again. He knew that the feathered lizard comment would not have gone well with her.

"She won't. Samar is more likely to eat Inman than a pigeon."

Both men laughed, truly relaxing for the first time this night.

"Are you truly going to send out another search party?" Harada finally asked after the laughter died.

"Yes. Garrick entrusted the girl to me and I should be the one out looking for her. I will organize a squad tonight and we will leave first thing tomorrow."

"I know I can't talk you out of it so I'll leave

and wish you luck now."

Vosloo rose with Harada and both men gripped each other in a fierce hug.

"Just remember to tell whichever lieutenant you leave in command that they should take my advice at times while you are away," Harada said as he leaned back and clapped Vosloo on the shoulder.

"Those Mind Bolts first started attacking Adhamh while we were flying around Daegarouf and that makes me wonder," Vosloo said abruptly as Harada was turning to leave.

The Wing Commander raised an eyebrow in surprise as he turned back to look at the Captain. "Why?"

Vosloo stepped away and started to step back and forth across the open area of his tent, reminding Harada of the Duke of Morcar's frantic pacing.

"The *Pydarki* do not tolerate anyone treading around that precious rock of theirs. Why did they allow the Icetigers and whoever made that bolt access to their mountain?"

"They most probably did not even know they were there. After all was it not you yourself who told the council that the Icetigers can appear from nowhere and attack?"

Vosloo stopped his pacing and raised a finger to his lips as if considering Harada's words. "Well, maybe you're right," he finally said and tried to give Harada a reassuring smile. "You had better go back to your own camp now. You have an early start tomorrow."

Harada turned back as he held up the tent flap to leave.

"Just don't do anything stupid Fraser."

The Captain smiled

"That's what men call bravery Harada."

"I know and many men have died because of it."

Then the Wing Commander was gone, the tent flap swaying in his passing.

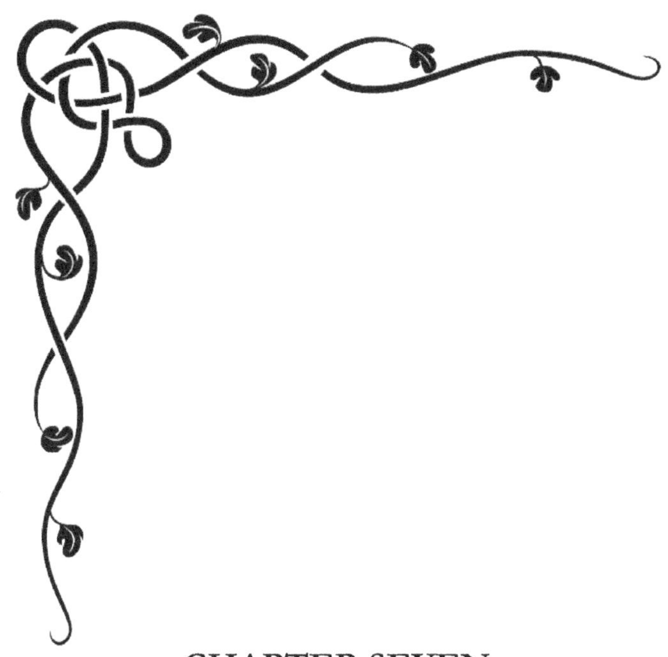

CHAPTER SEVEN

THE HUNT

The officer held a hand over his brow to cut the glare of the sun from his eyes. Beside him sat Captain Fraser Vosloo on a monster of a horse that was a twin to Prince Garrick's.

It had taken two days of careful tracking to find this location but now no further trace of their passage was seen. The officer did not know who his men were trailing except that they were on foot and there were at least six of them. His man had found a very well concealed camp in a large clearing about half a day's ride from here and it was only by chance that Hanton had found white animal hair on an oak where it had scratched itself.

"Lieutenant, what is your man doing?"

Dalon Peana started at the mention of his title. Beside him, Captain Vosloo moved to make himself more comfortable in the saddle. Dalon's eyes moved to watch Hanton as he quartered the ground before them. The rest of his men sat their horses behind himself and the Captain so as not to disturb what tracks might remain in the sea of grass.

"He is searching Captain, give him time."

Captain Vosloo leaned forward in his saddle, resting his arms on the high pommel.

"They get further and further away, the more time we spend looking." The Captain said more to himself than to Dalon, but the officer answered anyway.

"It is best that we spend time finding tracks, otherwise we might find ourselves on a wild goose chase by following the wrong signs. Then whoever we are tracking would be further ahead or lost to us completely."

"I know, I know," Captain Vosloo replied. "But I cannot stand the waiting and I do not want anything to happen to her."

"Then we are not just hunting Icetigers?" Dalon asked casually.

The Captain did not reply.

They waited a long while in silence until Hanton stopped suddenly, dropping out of sight to his haunches to study something hidden in the long grass.

Dalon stood in his stirrups to see if he could get a better look.

“Found anything?” he called.

Hanton continued studying the trace a moment longer before replying to his Lieutenant.

“Yep. A clear set of tracks heading straight into the plains, Lieutenant Peana. ”

The tracker stood up from his crouch and arranged his uniform back into place. It never seemed to fit the man who was too tall and too lanky to get any of his clothes to sit properly.

Hanton irritably brushed his mop of brown hair from his eyes before pointing towards the distant mountain range.

"In that direction, Sir."

"How old are the tracks?" Dalon called back.

"Over a day old at least."

"Are you sure it is theirs?" Captain Vosloo asked.

"Definitely. The paw print shows the same misgrown claw in it as that one I found at the camp site."

Hanton brushed his hands on his trousers as he walked back towards them. "There is something here that doesn't quite fit though I can't put my finger on it." He said more to himself though everyone heard it.

“What is it?” The Captain asked him.

Hanton jumped when he realized who was talking to him. The man touched a hand to his forehead as he bowed to Captain Vosloo.

“I don’t know, Captain. It’s just something…something doesn’t look right.”

“I see.” Captain Vosloo turned impatient eyes on Dalon.

“We move out, have your man lead the way.” Captain Vosloo heeled his horse into a trot.

Dalon turned to his men; raised his voice, “Move out.”

The horses came forward at a trot with Hanton quickly mounting and racing ahead to follow what little signs had been left behind.

They now ate trail rations in the saddle, as Captain Vosloo did not want to stop to eat and lose time. The only stops they had that day were when Hanton had to dismount to carefully study indistinguishable signs to make sure they were on the right track. After he was finished, they would move on again and it was always in the same direction – towards the Bhaglier Mountains.

Dalon rode silently next to the Captain who always stared ahead as if hoping to see something in the distance, not making any conversation as if that too would waste the time needed for this search.

As dusk approached Hanton rode into a small dell and immediately leapt from his horse to search the ground.

The rest of the group stopped on the lip of

the dell, watching Hanton combing the earth with the last rays of the setting sun.

"They were here last night, again no fire and only the barest trace that anyone had been here. There is something familiar about this Lieutenant Peana." Hanton said as he finished his search in the center of the dell.

"What is familiar?" Dalon asked as he dismounted from his horse.

"If I didn't know any better I'd say that we were tracking *Pydarki*."

The Lieutenant looked across his saddle to the Captain who had also dismounted and seen the disbelief that crossed his face.

"Devious bastards," Dalon heard the Captain say to himself.

"Captain?"

Vosloo flicked the stirrup up on his saddle and began to unhitch the girth strap.

"We camp here tonight and tomorrow we head straight to Daegarouf."

"Daegarouf!" Dalon said in shock. "We will not be allowed to go within a mile of its base without being turned back by their warriors. They do not like visitors."

"They will let us through." The Captain said. "They will let *me* through."

They rode on through the next day, only

stopping to rest the horses enough during the day to continue their journey.

Captain Vosloo pulled Hanton back to ride beside Dalon. He saw no need for a tracker now that he knew their destination. Dalon rode with the Captain who said little except to give commands and give curt answers to unwelcome questions.

That night, the Captain pulled a large glass bottle of wine from his saddlebags and poured out a generous helping into the cups of each soldier present. Just as the sun was setting he raised his cup in a silent tribute.

“We drink to the dead.” Captain Vosloo said and drank from his cup followed by the soldiers who stood silently around him. None knew who he drank to but the wine was much welcome.

“May they rest in peace.” Draining the rest of his cup, the Captain corked what was left in his bottle and returned it to his saddlebags. He then sat away from the campfires, away from the rest of the men, deep in his own thoughts.

When Dalon came to give the Captain his meal, he found him staring at an old folded piece of stained parchment that he hastily tucked back into his doublet pocket when he realized that the Lieutenant was approaching.

Dalon asked him no questions but sat and ate his meal with Vosloo. The man was troubled, and from Dalon’s experience the silent company sometimes helped ease a man’s mind.

The company rode hard for several days, eating trail rations when they could and bringing down game to supplement this when they were able.

Ahead of them loomed the Bhaglier Mountains and towering above the range was Daegarouf, it's crown covered by thick white cloud. Dalon inwardly shivered whenever it caught his eye. The Lieutenant had heard many stories about the mountain, some he knew to be blatant lies but others… he had heard other stories from men under his command. Men he knew could not lie to save their mothers. Men whose courage he would not question but at the mention of the mountain's name would turn to mush. He had seen many harsh things in his life – he was one of the few officers to have risen from the ranks – but nothing he had seen compared to those tales.

Hanton rode quietly beside him deep in his

own thoughts. Since the Captain had taken the lead, the tracker had nothing to do except to think, eat and sleep.

"How did you know that there were *Pydarki* in that group?" Dalon asked on the spur of the moment. He could only stand the ride in silence for so long.

The tracker jumped out of his thoughts with a start.

"I didn't say that I knew, I said it 'looks like' they were."

"Why did you think that?" Dalon asked, from the Captain's reaction to the news he had a feeling that Hanton had hit the nail right on the head.

The tracker shrugged. "The way the trail

was disguised. The technique used to cover or hide the tracks. It just looked like what the *Pydarki* use when they are out hunting." Hanton turned a quizzical expression to Peana.

"Why would the Captain want to hunt *Pydarki*?"

That's something I would like to ask him myself. But the Lieutenant only said, "He is not hunting *Pydarki*, he is hunting the Icetigers. Perhaps they have *Pydarki* prisoners."

The lanky man slowly nodded as if that made sense.

"When did you gain experience with *Pydarki* tracking techniques?" Dalon asked.

"About ten years ago. A group of Emperor's men went to the Mountain People for intensive training, a group of them came to us to learn some of our ways. I was with that lot for six months and I learnt more in that time than I did in three years apprenticed to the Emperor's Huntsman."

"They let you onto their mountain?" Dalon asked incredulously.

"No, of course not! They met us in the plains and then took us to another part of the ranges. One that they shared with the Arranians." Hanton stopped his explanation short at the mention of the Arranians. That seemed to bring out bad memories in the tracker. "They didn't want to treat us gently. If we were there to learn then we had to learn their way, and their way means leaving their youngsters to survive on the Borderlands by themselves for six months to see if they had correctly learned the survival skills from their elders. I do not like the Arranians."

Hanton withdrew into himself and dropped his horse back behind Dalon to ride alone with his own thoughts.

Dalon caught sight of the mountain again and shivered.

The snowdrifts were already deep and they were not even a third of the way up the mountain. Dalon had ordered his men to dismount and walk to make it easier on the horses in negotiating the snowdrifts. Each man and horse took it in turns leading the group, forging a path ahead through the snow to make it easier for the others to follow.

Everyone was uneasy.

They had expected to be met by the *Pydarki* two days back when they crossed into what the Mountain People thought was their border. But they had seen nothing. Nothing but grass and now nothing but snow.

Dalon had the creeping feeling that they were being watched. The only person who seemed not to worry was Captain Vosloo who determinedly forged his way ahead up the mountain, dragging the others along behind him.

It was now mid morning and Dalon was debating whether to wrap his horse blanket about him over the top of the three wool lined coats he already wore. Spring had just begun on the plains but had yet to reach the mountains that seemed reluctant to shed their white finery. High above them, a hawk circled, occasionally screeching its presence across the mountainside. Tails of hares could be seen disappearing into the brush and snow on either side of them, disturbing the many small mountain birds that lived among the bushes and brush.

Quickly looking behind him, Dalon sighed in relief when he saw only his own men. He had that feeling of being watched again. He glanced carefully around him but saw nothing unusual. Hanton now rode ahead with the Captain, looking for signs that others had passed that way. So far he had found nothing, the only tracks or markings that Hanton had found were those of hares, foxes, and birds.

The group came to a flat piece of ground, surrounded on three sides with thick evergreen conifers that cut out the icy cold wind that blew around the mountain and enough large rocks that protruded from the snow to make adequate seating.

"We will stop here for the night and maybe for the morning as well." The Captain said.

Dalon left Captain Vosloo and began shouting orders to his men who immediately jumped into action to build a suitable campsite.

As he stood near the center of the camp where the fire was being laid, Dalon felt those invisible eyes upon them all.

Night came quickly.

A large fire was built in the center of the camp with tents ringing it on the outside. The horses were picketed on the far side of the camp where the trees were the thickest, their tails turned to the harsh wind. The men had eaten their first hot meal in nearly a week. And, although it was cold, the men enjoyed the fact that they did not have to slog through the snow first thing the next day.

Captain Dalon had set the watches for the night over their meal and had then gone to bed. The feeling of being watched had stayed with him during the day and had intensified as soon as night fell. He had doubled the usual watch but, unusually, none of the men complained - maybe they felt something as well. He crept away early to his tent to rest and think.

Dalon could not sleep. Outside he could hear snoring coming from other tents and the gentle murmuring of the two men on watch by the fire. Occasionally, he could hear the footsteps of the outer guard as they stepped too close to the rear of his tent. Or the nickering of the horses on the picket lines as their opposites passed them on the other side of the camp.

He took a pull from his water container, he had refilled it using snowmelt from the fire before dinner.

Captain Vosloo had gone into his tent as soon as the evening meal finished. Dalon knew that something was worrying him but could not work up the nerve to ask him. It was not his place to ask the Captain his problems. Yet, reports from men who served with him on the border stated that he was an easygoing man who had a good rapport with those under his command. It was also said that he did not believe in hiding things from his command, that he trusted them to do what was right, as they trusted him. Dalon wished he knew what was going on but above all, he wished that he was off this One-forsaken mountain.

He leaned back in his bedroll, resting his head on his hands and stared at the canvas ceiling of his tent. The flames from the fire outside made flickering shadows dance against its white walls, but he still could not sleep. Thoughts whirled around in his head but would not settle, something the Captain had mentioned preyed on his mind but he could not remember what it was.

After a white of fruitless thinking, Dalon slowly drifted into sleep.

Dalon's eyes snapped open.

Something was wrong. But as he lay in the dark he could sense nothing. He could hear the snoring coming from the tents around him and the clink of metal as one of the men on watch moved on the far side of the camp. He was just imagining things.

Dalon reached across the tent to take a sip from his water skin when a noise outside stilled him. A snuffling sound came from the back of the tent. It sounded as if a large hunting dog was sniffing the trail of a fox that it had run to ground.

The Lieutenant slowly turned his head to the rear of his tent. The light of the campfire had died down and the inside of the tent was in near darkness. Outside, the half moon cast enough light to throw dark shadows against the canvas walls.

What Dalon saw nearly made him forget to breathe.

Snuffing unconcernedly at the rear of his tent was the perfect shadow of a large creature that reminded Dalon of both a cat and a dog and there was the strong smell of fox in the air.

Suddenly its nose poked under the tent flap showing a flash of pure white fur and a nose that reminded him of the large wildcats that roamed the plains to the south.

Dalon then heard the loud crunching of two pairs of boots as they approached his tent. "'Ere what's that?" he heard one say. The other guard realized what was happening.

"Lieutenant!"

Dalon watched as the nose disappeared back under the tent flap and a low feline growl answered the men.

"Don, watch out!' he shouted as he turned and grabbed his sword belt and, barely stopping to untie the flaps, bolted out the front of his tent.

He raced around to the opposite side that his men were approaching from, jumping unconsciously over guy ropes and spikes in the moonlight.

He heard querying shouts coming from the two men by the fire, asking what was going on. Dalon pulled his sword from its scabbard and tossed the belt to the ground as he came around the corner of his tent.

He halted dead in his tracks.

The creature before him was huge. The moon shadows that he saw against his tent had down played the size of this beast. It was the size of a small pony and was heavily built. At first glance, it looked like a grizzled white wolf but it had a short stocky tail and black tipped ears like the small tawny mountain cats that hunted in the western mountains. As he came around behind it, the beast turned to look at him. It's face looked like a mix between a wild dog and a cat.

It has the long nose of a dog that terminated in the V shaped nose that cats have. It panted like a dog but had sharp teeth and fangs like a cat.

The one thing that struck Dalon to the core of his being was the beast's eyes. They glared at him like blue ice and looked entirely too human. There was intelligence and cunning within those eyes.

He was struck by the feeling that the creature knew what he was thinking and could understand what was said around it.

The beast turned its head back towards the two men and growled low in its throat. Dalon heard footsteps and a loud curse behind him and knew without turning that the sentries by the fire had joined him. In a few minutes, the other pair of circuit sentries will be coming behind on the other side.

"What do we do Sir?" Don called across the creature.

"We'll wait for the other two to join us and then…"

The beast turned back to look at him as he spoke and he saw the human-like eyes narrow.

The Lieutenant took an involuntary step backward under that gaze. Dalon knew he looked death in the face. The creature dropped into a half crouch, never taking its gaze away from the Lieutenant; getting ready to leap.

Suddenly in the distance, the howl of a wolf echoed across the night and was answered immediately by several others. The white beast moved its gaze in the direction of the howls and spat, the wet globule hit the side of the tent and began to eat through the material.

The howls echoed once again and seemed to be closer. The creature swept its gaze over the men and then leapt up from between them to disappear into the trees and bushes that surrounded their camp.

The men stood facing the bushes with bared steel for what seemed like hours but were only a few minutes before relaxing enough to speak.

"What was that?" one man asked.

"Don't know, I don't want to know,"

another man answered.

Dalon turned from studying the hole left by the creature's spittle in his tent, he felt like running his finger around the edges of the hole but he dared not touch it.

"The watch will be doubled again tonight, Sergeant Don."

"Yes, Sir."

"I will inform the Captain of what has happened."

Dalon stood back as Captain Vosloo inspected the paw prints left in the snow, a soldier holding a lighted torch so that everyone could see. The prints looked to be that of a dog and were the size of a large dinner plate. They were clearly defined and showed that the creature was more massive than Dalon had imagined.

The Captain slowly stood, brushing away the snow that clung to his knee as he knelt.

"I've never heard of anything like this."

Hanton spoke up from beside the Lieutenant. "I have…the footprints I mean." He clarified when all eyes suddenly focused on him.

"As I told the Lieutenant, I lived for six months with the *Pydarki*. Once, when we were on patrol along the Arranian border closest to here we came across prints much like these. The young *Pydarki* that were with us got excited and immediately sent us Suenese back to camp. We never found out what it was about. Until now."

"Did you find any other tracks?" Dalon asked.

The tracker shook his head.

"This is it. There is not even a claw mark anywhere else around the camp."

Dalon turned to the Captain. "I've doubled the watch, I have a feeling that we will see them again."

Captain Vosloo glanced again at the footprint and the melted hole in Dalon's tent. "Soldiers should not have to be afraid of the local wildlife," Vosloo said and stalked off in the direction of the campfire.

There were no further incidents that night and the sun rose on an alert but uncertain camp. Dalon did not sleep that night, unlike the Captain who went back to his tent and, as yet has not come out. The Lieutenant glanced again at the Captain's tent and saw no movement.

The Center Watch had started the morning cooking pots and Dalon poured himself some tea from a kettle and seated himself on a rock beside the fire.

Nursing the warm mug more for its warmth than thirst, Dalon watched over a still quiet camp. The Lieutenant watched as the men worked the pots around the cook fire and sipped carefully at his tea.

Something niggled at the back of his mind, something was not right. That seemed to be happening a lot lately.

Dalon swept his eyes across the camp again. He saw the six men on patrol in the outer circuit, there were four men around the center, a pair of which was doing the cooking, and there was the pair of men guarding the horses.

Taking another sip of his tea, he glanced carefully around the circle of tents that surrounded the central fire. There were seventeen tents, his thirty men shared two to a tent and he and the Captain had single tents. Dalon's eyes rested on the Captain's tent. Its front tent flaps gave a gentle wave in the cold morning breeze and it took a moment for the Lieutenant to realize that inside it was empty.

He shot up from his rock like an arrow, barely missing his leg with burning tea as his mug dropped to the snow, and raced over to the tent's entrance to peer inside to make sure that his eyes weren't playing tricks on him. The men at the fire stopped what they were doing to finger the hilts of their swords uneasily.

"What's up Lieutenant?" one man called as Dalon turned to face them from the tent, a frown creasing his forehead. The tent was neat and ordered and the bedroll looked as if it hadn't been slept in. The Captain's pack was gone.

Dalon came slowly out of the tent and faced the men who crowded around him

“The Captain has disappeared.”

CHAPTER EIGHT

UNEXPECTED FRIENDS

The wispy smoke was barely noticeable above the thick trees that lined the mountain's side but the sharp eyes of the Haterle'magarten could see it clearly. It drifted lazily just above the snow-capped trees before it was broken up and blown away by the morning breeze.

Trar duly reported the sighting to Tayme.

'Who do you think it is?' Tayme asked. Their countless days searching had revealed no trace of either Kalena or the party who took her. He was desperate for any sign that might indicate where she was. and Tayme clung to the hope that she was still alive. Adhamh would have felt it if she had…

Tayme did not want to think about it. Somehow, a pair of Speaking Crystals know when one is destroyed.

Trar answered Tayme with a mental shrug.

'Let's go check it out just the same. It's the first time we've seen any sign of habitation since our search began.'

Slowly the five Hatar turned and glided low

against the trees, dipping, and diving along the undulating canopy in an effort not to be seen. As they slipped along the tree tops, Adhamh's silent presence loomed large in Tayme's thoughts. Ever since they had left Vosloo and their Wing on the Red Plains the Hatar had not been very forthcoming in what had exactly happened when he was knocked from the sky. He only repeated what he had told Trar the day they found them on the grasslands.

And when Tayme asked about what he meant by his comments on the Captain, Adhamh remained unusually silent. Over the last few days, the Hatar had withdrawn so much into himself that he hardly said a word to anyone.

And who could blame him? The Hatar had lost someone who he has shared every moment of his life with for the past eight years.

Tayme could understand.

With Kalena gone he felt as if a part of him had been ripped out and hidden away. Now all Tayme had to do was to find it again.

'Trar, see if you can find somewhere close by where there is enough room for us to land. We humans will approach on foot and see if we can get a look at what's there.'

Trar quickly began to scan the forest ahead of them, her red feathered head quickly moving back and forth looking for a large enough break in the green.

'There is a suitable place over to the left Tayme. It does mean a bit of a walk for you to that campsite.'

Tayme gave Trar's neck a good scratch. *'After all this time in the air, we need the exercise.'*

The group veered a little to the west, following Trar's directions.

It was a tight fit but all the Hatar managed to land and bunch up in the large clearing that had obviously been cleared by fire as blackened stumps of cracked and broken trees poked clear above the snow. It sat just to the south west of the campfire and even with the distance on foot it was close enough for the Hatar to respond quickly to any call for help.

Even in the tightness of the clearing Tayme noticed that Adhamh managed to stand to one side with enough separation between him and the other four Hatar to look like an outcast. He will have to try and get Adhamh out of the shell he is hiding behind but that will have to wait until later.

Tayme quickly dismounted along with the others and grabbing his sword belt and a brace of daggers quickly called the three other riders to him.

"Make sure you have your swords ready and some daggers close to hand. We don't know who is beyond by that fire but whoever had attacked Adhamh had firstly done so in this area." Tayme swept an arm around him, taking in all the trees, bushes, snow and the great mountain of Daegarouf.

"The bastards still could be around lurking where the *Pydarki* cannot detect them. For all, we know this campfire could just be a group of *Pydarki* out on a picnic. Even so, just follow me and do as I say. Got it?"

The three Flyers nodded.

Quickly, the group crossed from out of the morning sunlight and into the sheltered gloom of the evergreen branches. This high up on the mountain they still grew strong and thick and as the Flyers moved deeper into the trees they found that the snow barely reached the ground. Dried leaves and pine needles crunched and shattered underfoot and birds called out from snow-clad branches hidden above them.

Instinctively, Tayme and his Flyers knew in which direction lay the campfire. All Flyers have a good sense of direction. It was well known that you could blind fold one, spin them around and lock them in a chest and they would *still* be able to point out North. It was one of the gifts given by the

Krytal.

They loped quickly through the trees nimbly side stepping gnarled tree roots, fallen branches and other obstacles that the forest had cultivated.

At the head of the group, Tayme was the first to hear the loud crashing and cursing of several men ahead of them. Quickly holding up a hand, Tayme signaled to the Flyers who immediately stopped and crouched down between two large trees and peered ahead into the gloom.

Tayme could see nothing at first but the sounds of crashing footsteps and the occasional cursing told him that there were at least ten men coming in their direction.

'At least they *are* men and not IceTigers,' Tayme thought and turned to look back at his people.

His eyes widened in shock.

Behind them stood two men, sword points resting casually on the backs of both Jill and Treaer. The two Flyers dared not look back and had their hands raised above their heads where everyone could see them.

“Lieutenant, look what we have here.”

Suddenly the crashing and cursing stopped and Tayme watched as silent men stepped towards them through the trees.

The man who spoke was too lanky to get any of his clothes to sit properly and he had a thick mop of brown hair that tried to hide most of his face.

Tayme looked at the man standing next to

him.

The man looked like he had been born for the military. He filled out his uniform well and had his black hair cropped short under the Lieutenant's cap he wore. Tayme recognized the colors the officer wore at his neck. He was one of Vosloo's men.

"Yes, Hanton. But what, pray tell, are they doing here?"

The Lieutenant's sword was lifted from Treaer's back and quickly sheathed. The other sword disappeared with equal haste.

Tayme slowly rose to his feet. How had they come behind them so quietly? The other three Flyers were slow to follow suit but jumped up quickly after an angry hand movement from Tayme.

Tayme took a deep breath and then bent his back into a formal bow. The other Flyers did the same. A Freeman Officer had addressed them.

"I am Kral Kalar, Acting Wing Commander of Second Wing, First Flight. We saw camp smoke and have come to investigate."

"What are you doing out this way in the first place?" Tayme heard the clinking on metal as the Lieutenant laid a relaxed hand about the hilt of his sword.

"Captain Vosloo sent us out searching for the Icetigers that have taken Kalena Kalar, our Wing Commander."

Tayme stayed ducked in his bow as the Lieutenant stood silently in thought.

"We have also been sent on a search for

Icetigers," he said eventually. "But he was also searching for a woman. Do you know why your Wing Commander is so important to him?"

Tayme shook his head in reply.

"Pity. Well, stand up then, we can't be doing this all day," the Lieutenant said with a flick of his hand. "Talk to me as you would any man. We don't need any of this bowing and scraping out here."

The Flyers slowly released themselves from their bow and glanced uneasily about them.

"I am Lieutenant Dalon Peana." Peana held his hand out to Tayme.

"I am Kral Tayme." Tayme took the Lieutenant's hand and shook it warmly. This mountain is a strange place to meet unexpected friends.

"Is the Captain here with you?" Tayme asked as he quickly looked at the faces around them and did not recognize anyone.

"He was last night but this morning he was gone. When we saw the Hatar approaching we thought he might have arranged for a pick up."

"Do you mean he is missing?"

"I mean the man has disappeared without a trace from our camp," the frustration in the Lieutenant's voice struck a chord in Tayme. His brief experience with the Captain gave him the same feeling. The Lieutenant then told Tayme briefly about the events of the night before and of the Captain's persistence that the *Pydarki* were involved in the attack. In his turn, Tayme told

Peana what happened the day of the attack and their fruitless search afterward.

"Perhaps our parties should join forces, after all, we are both out here for the same reasons. Combined we should both be able to find your Captain, our Wing Commander, and those blasted IceTigers," Tayme said as he finished his story.

"Sounds like a fine idea. Come back to our camp and we'll organize arrangements over a hot breakfast."

CHAPTER NINE

WHO AM I?

She felt rough hands pawing at her and then felt something sawing away at her leg straps. But she was only vaguely aware of her surroundings. She tried to open her eyes but could not. It was as if her lashes were glued shut and the furious pounding in her temples made her give up the idea of opening her eyes altogether.

Then strong arms lifted her from the saddle and she felt herself lowered gently to the ground where a fur blanket was wrapped about her.

Immediately she snuggled into it as she realized just how cold it was. Drifting to sleep, she could hear the frantic buzzing of voice messages flying around her mind. She could not quite hear them but she relaxed in her sleep knowing now that she was safe.

To Be Continued in

Part 4

The Enemy Within

Continue the season and get cool stuff!
If you liked *The Kalarthri*, *The Dream Thief and The Awakening* you will love *The Enemy Within.*

Thank you so much for reading and I hope to see you again.

Thank you for reading my book. If you enjoyed it, won't you please take a moment to leave me a review on Amazon?

THE KALARTHRI

The Way to Freedom, Book One

"This Hatar Kalar has more natural Talent than any Second Born found in the Empire."

Every ten years the Imperium Provosts travel the provinces of the Great Suene Empire and take every second born child as the property of the Emperor. His Due for their continued protection.

Kalena, taken from her family and friends finds herself alone and scared in the imperial Stronghold of Darkon. And when she cries out to the darkness for help, Kalena is shocked when it answers her back.

Book 2: The Dream Thief

Book 3: The Awakening

<u>HOWLING VENGEANCE</u>

John McCall Mysteries, Book One

John McCall just wanted to get a surprise for his men. Instead he got a disemboweled body.

A man is arrested for the murder but McCall is sure that they have the wrong person.

And when McCall starts digging around for the truth, he unearths a whole lot more than he bargained for.

Howling Vengeance. A supernatural mystery in the Old West.

Available now at your favorite Online Bookseller

THE ENCLAVE

The Verge, Book One

Katherine Kirk lived only for vengeance.

Vengeance against the man who destroyed her home, her family and her life.

Sent on a babysitting mission to Junter 3, RAN officer Katherine Kirk, finds herself quickly embroiled in the politics between the New Holland Government and the Val Myran refugees claiming asylum.

After an Alliance attack Kirk and her team hunt the enemy down and discover that they have finally found the lair of the man they have been searching for…

And the captive who has been waiting patiently for rescue.

"What would you do to the man who destroyed every important person in your life?"

W i n t e r ' s M a g i c

Book One of The Order

Kaitlyn Winter is biting at the bit to become an active agent for the Restricted Practitioners Unit. And on her first day in the job she is thrown into a virtual s**t storm (to put it nicely).

First, she gets targeted for Assassination by The Sharda's top assassin

Second, her Werewolf best friend decides that her being '*Straight*' means she can't protect herself and places her in protective custody

Third, the love of her life still won't notice her existence and the Tempus Mage who's set to keep an eye on her is infuriatingly attractive....

You can find out more information and sign up for Hayley's monthly newsletter on her website
http://www.hmclarkeauthor.com/

ABOUT THE AUTHOR

In a former life, H M Clarke has been a Console Operator, an ICT Project Manager, Public Servant, Paper Shuffler and an Accountant (the last being the most exciting.)

She attended Flinders University in Adelaide, South Australia, where she studied for a Bachelor of Science (Chem), and also picked up a Diploma in Project Management while working for the South Australian Department of Justice.

In her spare time, she likes to lay on the couch and watch TV, garden, draw, read, and tell ALL her family what wonderful human beings they are.

She keeps threatening to go out and get a real job (Cheesecake Test Taster sounds good) and intends to retire somewhere warm and dry – like the middle of the Simpson Desert. For the time being however, she lives in Ohio and dreams about being warm…

You can find out more information and sign up for Hayley's monthly newsletter on her website –
http://hmclarkeauthor.com
http://eepurl.com/SPy61

Or catch her on Twitter - **@hmclarkeauthor**

Made in the USA
Las Vegas, NV
09 June 2022